Gasping For Air

By Robert Clifford

Designed by Jesse Beam
Published by Jesse Beam

This book is dedicated to my beautiful Children,

Peter Begrowicz Dolan Clifford

Scott William Hayes Clifford

and the loving animals in their life that now guide

them from Heaven

Marquerita, Londie, Pangor, Nibbler

Foreward

On first reading Bob Clifford's poetry, as a Southern woman, I thought that if Flannery O'Connor had been a Northerner and had written poetry it might resemble Bob Clifford's. Populated by outcasts, the marginalized, the poor and dispossessed, and sometimes the grotesque, Clifford's poems seek a rough redemption that is rooted more in hope for something better than in any circumstance in which his characters, including himself, find themselves. These people live hardscrabble lives, survivors on "the backstreets of Cambridge where Harvard does not live." The poems are mostly dark and create a sense of oppressive futility and desperation, but, here and there, small glimpses of human spirit suggest that not all is bleakness and desolation. In these deeply personal poems, Clifford grapples with the death of his mother, his overbearing and finally absent father, his waning Catholic faith, and his developing deafness. The poems give a strong sense that Clifford's relationship with his mother is much more complicated than his relationship with his "governor father" whose heart is "empty." His father comes and goes and dies before Clifford's mother who has the last word, commenting that if his father knew he had been buried "under the sun and a hill with grass he'd be rolling over in his grave looking for the first place to have a drink." In this landscape of the industrial North, Clifford often yearns toward the West as a symbol of openness and possibilities for redemption. While many poems point to the despair of hopelessness and the lack of positive change in familiar places like the gas station and the school, others look for a way forward despite the despair. In these urban passages of youth, the mind "seizes which way to the meadow to catch a ride with the butterflies." Clifford is often caught between his "haunted past" and future and, in moments of hope, carries the past into the present where "stems stand up to hope." Death figures large as a theme in these poems, but it does not always triumph. That the final poem in this collection is a tribute to a young woman kidnapped and murdered just off a university campus is fitting. As in many of the other poems in the collection, evil personified plays a large role in this poem, but it doesn't prevail. Like Clifford's other characters, Brook exists on the margins, "On the West side of the pit." Yet even in the darkness of her murder, we find hope, because, in the end, the devil, the monster captures her innocence but not her. She, like so many of the other women in Clifford's collection, including his mother, is much more than what happened to her, what others did to her. She is still herself, fully human, and at last beyond the reach of harm and death.

Susan M. Shaw, PhD
Professor of Women, Gender, and Sexuality Studies
Director of the School of Language, Culture, and Society
Oregon State University

Sitting in a bar thinking about
the sights that have not
changed

the gas station
the school
the church
the friends

kids on the corner
the cops
even the field that I used to
lay
in and cry

Going Home

Mother is still dead
The house the governor father
sold And enriched - again

Our life on a forced march

4 times not counting the

Ones I do not know about

What did mother really think

What does my dead father think

What did my alive father think

mother is still dead on the porch couch
Her eyes opened curl straight - up
Still no teeth
Still no live mother
Still no picture

Standing on a bridge
a pond that is old and dirty
Saint Michael's stares on my
right side
looking down at the police
and fireman under water
trying to find a young bloated
lifeless boy
who had traveled from a village
three thousand miles away to
find
happiness in a new world of
unwanted adventure
A priest arrives with his virgin
face and hands
the parent's young wrinkled faces
from work not despair
rosary beads of hell
the silver tank is first
with bubbles
an endless black body rises like
a
volcano
to the eyes that watch
his right hand of senselessness
wave
for the protections
as the rosary beads break and
the
people go home for supper.

Down the road in a valley from

heaven

a small town with
rocking chairs sits idle
fire places burn slow
old man remembers world war I
a bar with pictures of men
from world war II
breath motionless
a cold beer is poured
a pop inhaled
a cop laying cards
a chair full of gentlemen
further down the road a woman
sits in a kitchen with the
Virgin Mary beside her pictured
son
with a cold cup of coffee
she looks out the window
into a converted hayfield
laced with fog.

Early

The midmorning ride

Not sunrise, not sunset
The driver - a figure from the hard hat manual
Balding, trying to grow a beard.
He had hot air for breakfast the weather and
them
he lost sleep over both.
Money his demand,
Impolitely I slip him his demand.
Uncomfortable as my mind reaching for my
pen
The stripes in the road a duck with his
head in the water.
Besides a road that is refinished more
than me.

Going home to the Assabet Valley
Going home to the 617 area code
Going home to the new area code
978

Walking down another street where home is not
Roseland, Main St. Pope St. Church St.
Lincoln St. Central St. Sommerville
Cambridge Hull, Cape Cod, Columbia
Point, Watertown Carried west by the
Boston and Maine
Carried out by my thumb
Rt. 9 going east and west

My other half carried out by army
Learning to read and write with the
Puerto Ricans, Portuguese and
Blacks

My other half in the desert not on a

Wagon train

Leaving mother for Tahoe

Coming home again

The dwarf was a spy

For the funeral home

Mother's ash tray still

On the dashboard of

Isabel's Impala

Oh Dad oh Mom
you sentence your children
for crimes of morality
oh church, if you did not exist
would we have been cleansed
from your sins?
what number bus did he
get on?
he left again
on a dark night in a dark town
that he found because of the county jail
then sweeping floors for God
when he rolled back down
the stairs
clutching, grabbing, reaching
for his empty heart.

Across the field and up the

hill,
beyond the virgin pinewall
lies the cold dirt I fell in
after being shot in the neck
by a nobody with a powder
puff
gun.
Only six not even a life.
I ran down the hill
screaming I was dead,
only the holes in the clothes
and vocal cords
carried any truth.
My father overweight
coke bottle glasses
gray grease slick hair,
he did not open the door
long enough for the
wind to hit him.
The coat, sweater, shirt
peeled
off.
what a day in six years to come
home
he gargles.
The warm water soap
killed dreams of being dead.
The father sits down again
with his back again
to my face
while the water dries
on my back
across the field and up the
hill
beyond the virgin pinewall
lies the cold dirt I fell in.

The High Street school
on top of the hill
above Saint Michael's
when it was alive it
processed good little
boys and girls
from homes that had
pictures
of John F. Kennedy and
Pope John XXIII -
the Odd Ones had Richard
Nixon
the odd ones sat in front
with answers and smiles
the ones who had a sense of
humor sat in back of the
sacred
first two rows
and were not asked for
answers -
like the boards that now
cover
the windows of the school
that could not process
more than two rows of
answers and smiles.

George told me my old

rat-

trap house burned down
along with the ground
fair amount of looking up
to adult world was
spent in between the
leaves and grass
until we would roll off
the stone wall and end on
oar
heads figuring how come
god did not like nice
catholic
boys with food stamp
supplies
to squirm down your
throat
a dead rat in the bathroom
people downstairs with a
broken piano
top bunk bed provided the
longest sleep from noise
the eyesore
of one street and town is
gone...
along with innocence

Across the street sat a

midget.
on a porch built by a
yankee father
endless days the black iron phone
went
click click click,
after her toothpick fingers
breathing out of control
on the last white hole
her teeth clacked together
with her bridge mouth
waiting for the the wrinkled
rings to cease.

The Brookline Lunch
the morning after being
shipwrecked the night before,
a cook with a duck's ass and
a Camel hanging on the side,
of the callous lips like a
plug for a dam
two waitresses with black
tbeehive
hairdos,
white pancake faces,
maybe from the old country
or just the backstreets of
Cambridge where Harvard lives
not.
We sit in the rear,
not sure who is a cop or crook
or both.
A man slumps at the counter,
his insides start to come out
call his brother
call the priest
call the fireman
the brother comes
the priest does not.
the firemen come with plywood,
the twenty-six eyes are waiting.

After food and cigarettes kill her
bones traveled west and did not come
back
buried a dead bird
rode a yellow bus without my other half
bones hated the same teacher too
where the wooden footbridge could
not change a pair of blue see
through pants with no underwear.

The night passage of youth
when the eyes are not opened
by you
across the street the old lady
waits for one more of something
while the dog wants to go for a
walk
crawling again inside
the lights do not come on
while your feet shuffle
on the floor inside and out
the black sky of your ceiling
collapses -
crawling out again to the top
on the way back to the flower
the moon hides behind the
clouds
as your mind seizes
which way to the
meadow to catch a ride
with the butterflies

Leaving Porter

Square
going West
the train stops
somewhere in the
snow,
stepping off into the
night.
after riding the rails
into the dark west
on a patch of dirt
that speaks of the
life that it had
inherited the grip
that would never let
go-
when your pulse
becomes
a permanent resident
of the past
from the ride in the
night.

Laying in the white bed with
the curtains flapping back and
forth a nurse wants me to leave
the building its time to go

no ride going west
no phone call from the west
how do I get west
can I hear or not hear
dirty underwear again
I cannot change them

waiting for word about the tide
while the white coats, white
dresses
and white people
call each other about the white
boy
of trash, who has no ride
who does not understand
how being real white
will not be achieved by duress
of their beds
that they rent to you-
no ride west
back to bed
that is no longer white

To John R. Clifford Cpl. USMC
Vietnam, December 1966 - January 1968

My brother who was in the fox
hole
wrote and told me he wouldn't write
me when I ended up in one myself.
cause I never wrote him.
never understood why he said that
did not know that I did not write
I never understood what it was to
have a brother in a fox hole so we did
not
talk
I discovered
foxholes were not just for movies
it was too late for me to fill the hole
with letters or talk-
while the invisible letters
stacked up

Sitting in my friend's kitchen
telling his mother and aunt what
a nice neighborhood they live in
sweet smell of Greek food
nice young niece sewing the cob
webs
clearing out our heads
after a fulfilled night
the wrath of Mayor Daley
my mouth a sand dune
a brick arrives uninvited
twelve eyes survey the damage
one pair looks at me-
yes, you are correct I do not speak
Greek
a solemn moment of truth
that carried the Brick through
the window, on to the Island
floor of their pilgrimage from
their God.

My uncle took me to a bar that had
my father's footprints
moons, drinks, bets, old whores ago
the floor fits into.
bartender looks as if he should have
been a priest.
me a baby amidst the 1,000 years of
duty
done by the twenty people on the
stools
no road now to see that now or later

The coach gave me a number to

cover
my eyes only saw his lips move
the lights shining
the bodies placid as apples in the
trees
black and white stripes yelling to
play
I walk back on the court of
harwood
the minute then the seconds are
gone
along with a man I never saw
my head down and gone
like a stubbed toe you try to walk

Standing on a curb outside an
emergency room
old man grayed goatee
toe through one old shoe
his brother with five heart attacks
and
his last tonight at 8:40 p.m.
my useless book
I ask him if he was okay
a tear answered as he pointed
to the scrubs across the parking
lot that had died
the wind was light as his eyes
on a journey
the thing taxpayers paid for to be
carried
away clean disappears
the callous lips of pall malls cracked
a hanky a hundred years old
knuckles shaped like pinballs,
square knots, blown up boulders
the old security guard to talk
baseball
the goatee road map face
pointed to his sister-in-law
a trooper.

On mornings when my tongue

and
teeth could not meet
with my cheeks and lips
to say good morning or
hello
the world would begin to rattle
in slow motion
the throat plugged
the face red
the knees weak
innocent eyes from faces
with mouths that flow
like computers - would stutter
also.

I grew up one day and found

out
about adolescence-
my neighbor the fatman with
the
red face and butt in his mouth
found out that I found out
told me still be a kid
or he was going to break my
head open

Riverside Park
Hudson, Massachusetts,
America
under the lights young men
of the insulated world gather
to beat their dreams
out from other dreams
the hot chocolate is hot
the hot dogs, steamed
the police steamed
the mist from dreams of the
river
settles above the
fifty yard line
while the hawks come as
people
to watch people
collide like hawks.

Old lady dwarf sits by the
porch door with her two
telephones
she would yell to the kids
democrats plus jews
eat a pint of ice cream
funeral home phone rings
she shut up, say her stories
to the family
call the hearse
then picks up her phone and
with a smile to Helen her friend
relays the good news.

ON BEING DEAF

If you could only hear what I see
you would notice the people who
talk with rocks in their mouths and
listen with pencils in their ears
and accuse you of not listening to
their gobbledygook.
my ears not built for lazy brain cells
neither my eyes
my soul was made from a womb
that gave me no jail bars to see
beyond my eyes

Driving my '63

white
Chevy up a tree-
lined
street,
tapping away to The
Temptations,
dreams,
being horny, young,
a new family.
the cars in front
begin to swerve-
a little pup did
not want to get out
of the road
as his head thumped
off the bottom of
my
oil tank
my chilling spine
pulls the car over

A cold winter
night

without the warmth
of love or your
favorite tree as your
strawberry Sundae
melts in
June before you even
get to drink the
cold water for the rush
to the head

A fire swallowed another building

in blue, red, orange and black
red trucks came running like foxes
people from the old country
worked in the hut of hollow wood
condemned
across the small polluted river
people grab their strong boxes
of paid bills and future cash
which they can only see after they
die
it was Halloween and my friend
needed a
trick or treat
as the blue red orange and black
settled in

Behind the tractor plow
Walking
The black rows of dirt
Gasoline stinks the air
Corn seeds that grease your hands
Dropping, grinding them into
God's stomach
Black rubber tires
The engine crawl forward
Size 6 1/2 feet inching along
Up and down
The rows
God's stomach must be empty
Big black tires do not hint
The sky looks down
Sitting Bull speaks from the
clouds
Reminding the trespassers
on the Black soil that they have raped
without God's blessing.
To feed
The invaders who
Escaped the Bible
To use as a weapon

Black Valiant picks me up

hitching
white man blue eyes coke-bottle
glasses
books on his cloth patched seat
engine in tune with the scenery
nothing too loud
what do you do with yourself.
a student.
I have over
5,000 books in my personal library
sell insurance also to get ahead.
then I stood on the side of the road
with
my mouth shut.

A train that is silver but black with smoke

moves like a hula hoop down the cracks of

the rails

people from another job and life sit there

and stare between the lines of newspapers

wondering when a train accident will finally

take place

a black kid sits on the toilet at the rear

wondering if the hook nose conductor with

retread eyelids will hunt him for the $1.25

we ramble rumble to Boston

the black boy does not have to pay

my pants are dirty.

Beer bottles on the table
smoke circling the air
the bartender stuffing
popcorn
in his mouth
Mary, the has-been cheerleader,
sits
with her legs spread
Arty, the barfly, wonders
when was the last World Series
Rookie gambler counts money he
does not have
faces from the great war of thirty
years
ago stare through the patrons
Martha, the old lady from the rest
home
dreams about walking into the
water.

Bus Station in Toledo

The Clock reads 2:59 A.M.

Book machine took my money
W.F. Burke is always saying read, read, read
I tried to, it wouldn't let me read

No. 2 was the slot
push the round black button
I pushed once, twice, three times.
No book, No book, No book

Never got the name of it either

So this is Toledo at 2:59 A.M.

always count on Greyhound

Blinding white lights
Brown checker linoleum

A sign to sit, A sign to ask questions

section to sit, sections to stand.

The 422 Chevy that brought me is gone, the thing that

brought me to the machine that wouldn't
let me read.

Buttons on a flat surface
you push them down
while you sing the
blues to a voice you
cannot see buttons of
numbers can take you
anywhere while your
feet are waiting to go

Black numbers in round
circles have broken and
created love affairs while the
eyes no longer see victims.

Pardon me your honor I am nervous
lawyer said take your time
my father was in this courtroom
5,110 days ago and then did
365 days for not understanding himself
now his son stands before the same
man
Ralph the cop who taught one son
religion
with one hand and beat the brother with
the other hand said I do tell the truth
of bruises, cuts, size 12 shoes on
someone's
neck and pulling hair
young punk prosecutor trying to
eyeball
me
all the black and blues visible
the judge said I see
the cop said I only know what I saw-
that is true too.

Fingertip fills the crater
On the neck where the
Metal of a pellet
Reached into my life line
Spinning my mind forward
One of the four seasons
My eyes from the past and the future
Cannot sense the day and the faces
The pine tree wall standing over the field
Hindsight not available
The foreign hands of father tend to the virgin
wound
The crater a shadow of the moon
The shadow that follows everywhere
Through the departure of dad
Bone's echo off the western mountains
That it was not the back
OR a disease of the skin
It was a human
Who missed.

Hollow Dreams

Lonely as the night you first

Slept without being rocked-

Lonely as the dreams you have imagined

In the center of hollowness trapped

Nowhere to go but in further,

Circling in, winding out

The reel is stuck

Helpless as a fish, gasping for as little air

For what little life and dreams

It has until the unknown - -

It wants out, you want out

Nowhere to go once again

Funny isn't it?

We were all sure at one time, weren't we?

Of going up sooner or later

The fish is gasping still-

Not to go up or down

Just hoping to feel once again

The open streams.

I wanted to buy flowers today
That colored the air
A smell that would carry me back
Up the road
I want to say that you bought them for me
While my pores sweat against a picture of my
mind
Dripping down my face
Through the cavity of
My chest
To the center of the magic well
That endless magic well
Praying for your soul to unshackle and leap
The flowers blossom again
Walking back down the road
From up the road
The pores have dried
The stems
Stand up
To hope

I went for another hearing test today
not like the cold subway winds of Boston
to the Mass General
when I wore sneakers three hundred sixty five days a
year-
no lunch money just a free hitch
back to the second floor walk-up where
it all began after the migration from
the cold cement of the east to virgin
hills of the west-
and the gentle bars that serve men-
as if they are being breast fed
I went for another hearing test today
no more huhs and whats
no contempt for destiny
or the lips that I could not follow
except
when drunk-
no more thinking ocean when they talk mountains
I sit now with my legs uncrossed

My eyes crawl through the black

box,
The sculpture of your bones
That lifts your face
Not talk to you
My hands cannot follow
My eyes
The mirrorless canal
That connects
You to me
Diving into my brain
The pound symbol
Banged, banged
Banged
Surfing the vain wires
Sounds of your face
Dangles me
The wind howls
Violence of the
Ocean
Mountains get
Smaller
We grow into each other
Out of the black box
That will sculpture a soul.

My passion grows everyday for you-
  Shadows cover the sun
Stepping over the route of cracks from
the
Map that left us benign.

Crawling out of the womb backward
into
Life
Ascension to civilization
  A thoughtless thought
  The snakes have grabbed the
  leftovers

Passion of your soul
When the lights
Come on you are not there

Your eyes have not betrayed the
picture After many storms that have
invaded your Innocence from the sea

Walking backwards toward you
brings Back a future that missed the
next stop

The path of the sun circles
The deer being trapped by Indians

Swimming in a polluted

pond
Orange water no
bubbles As the
chicken's heads roll
Without love
They can still dance
No takers
A search continues in
a Storm that flies non-
stop In a cranial of
vessels that Weave the
highway of Black
clouds that circle
The sight and sounds
Of a blurred facade
Crawling out of the bubble
From the top leaving the
Bottom untouched.

The boulders of muscle on young
boys who leave mothers apron strings,
in front of one hundred thousand savages
whose
bodies will never be as beautiful
to break
the boulder of boys
move sweetly
forward, sideways, up, down, across
picking a number to crucify
because they cannot hit their fathers-
while the fathers cry in dark barroom
corners
mothers pray-
the young warrior searches for a chief
who will never meet him.

To Jay, Love Always

The volcanoes ripped your body apart
Two pieces
Of skin rubbing against each other
Through the exit black hole of waste
Everyday in the mirror
Your face
Your search, touched and sensed
Traveling the bottom road
Did you ever enjoy sex?
The lava rips and sucks
Each organ apart
Your heart still a virgin
The boiling rocks now pound the organs
To decimate, destroy, intimidate
So they wish
Not to return in your
Next life-
Laying there like a bag of brown bones,
The whites of your brown eyes sucking
Morphine like candy did you budget this
The gray dirt that you will be in the brown bottle
You did not know the consequence of your search for love
As your petulant bitchy self crawled inside of
You and killed you.

The Day I Returned To Hudson High School

Standing before my haunted past
Wondering where I would have sat
Wondering why I was asked to sit

The dictator today
One day in 12 years
A chance to correct all the falsehood

Fall of 1967 the final rush began

Three falls to go, two summers to go

left to the then unknown.

I the little brother, the five minute older twin
Bouncing Round ball, dreamt me through and got
me through
Running over the leaves and streams
Kept me lonely and a loner

Stuttering to my peers, never mind my pets, with-
drawn to a forest of
my mind

Junior year did not hear the leaves crackle,
the time was a reckon I felt it as my toes
went numb and my body froze I wanted to piss
my pants

Pretty girls talked to me I thought
My thoughts could not talk back
Oh God
I missed a call in roundball it cost the school
the game.

Senior year a picture of me for the book
Why?
I mumble "that is not me"
Tour of Viet Nam was over
for my family now.
My war just began.
I am afraid it is me.

46

The winter came and went as fast as my 18th year began
in April of 1970
June came and left me with a piece of paper that burns to
live my live with, last of the class they told me,
never knew I belonged to a class
The haunting past can end like a dream that whipped you

                                                    scared
you and beat you.

The virtues that they beat into you were the end.

            My brain cells traveled your
            road My soul dragged your
            paths
            My tears messed up your class
            rooms My presence a mystery

47

The wind is snapping tonight on
the
outside
while the branches shake their
sins
loose
the birds huddle
while the gladiators hump
themselves into position
to block out being sifted by
Gods snapping cruel cold wind
that is beating nature because
of the fools he created

The yard stares at me
The grass brown yellow
Petulant
Heavy wind stuck
African heat
A fence no longer a wall
Twigs do not crack
The ground is full

I have not waltzed on the roads of
Maine
Bobby Wade from the High Street
School
A son of the town saints had his
tonsils
Removed and died.
Railroad tracks that carried coal
West and east across Bruce's
A dead pond brown and orange
Currents circle into a black spiral
Walking on the outside rail
On a trestle
A cross stares
At the virgins.

Walk along one lane
Going neither way
The squirrel scampers by
A shadow reflects
Your soul
The shadow does not reveal
How the sun ponders on your
Future
One lane going neither south or
North or East or West
Travels to the seasons
Nor foliage
Or hope
Crying the yelps of the wolves
Brings a primal shot to the
Top.

She took me home to her house
with the room upstairs to the
rear where you can see the no
parking
sign
the carpet was old as the paint
the walls did not even have a
shadow or sound
the sheets were wrinkled
her toes dirty
she laid her body on the bed
like it would move what was not
there, her and me.

Walked through the back
door
down the broken stairs
down the hilly broken
driveway
to a side walk
that made me skip gaps
as I wander forward
grabbing the ledges of a
stonewall
trying not to look back
at the cracked house

Notches that pile on the

blades
that twist and cuddle the black
soil
that sucks oiled seeds
that will sprout
a cornfield along a road
under a virgin sky
on top of manure
sliding forward waiting for
repent
until paws gather
a crop to see inside out.

Blue vein legs lumpy hands
And tight faces
Waltz through the frosted air
Packing red apples
That curve their hand half a day
Red stems crawl down the silver
tray
1-2-3-4-
a marching band of refugees
fill the ice chest on wheels
cold ladies looking cold
walking slow loading slow
the frosted white air
circles white breath
that gets smaller

A soul relieved of her
duty
tongues begin to move from
the
hymns
eyes down cast to the relief
of
their duty
the right church, a bad pew
the dim rays that nurse
the white knuckle faces
while the thin lip soldier of
god
taps a melody of departure
the old bird went kicking,
and threatened to stay
longer
her last invitation was
ten years ago
that was a mistake

Work

Punched the clock 7:15 a.m.
Sinus still dry from yesterday's
steam from the tubs
tubs ancient labor
pulley to carry, pail dip into,
dip out of tub.

Hola! To fellow workers
Azores where they come from
1/4 of the joint all from the Old Country
Me wonder why they come for this I
wonder
why I come back for more

Piece, Piece more pieces done

more mucho dinero
Mold the iron 110%, Mold, Mold
Dipping my pails into tub and out.

Ever make four dollars an hour maybe
three weeks vacation too.
immigrants run work hard America can't
be that much of a dream.
My dream is get out of the shops
the town, the country

Job doing something for my arms coaches
never
could do.
Big aims, hard and yet soft
Ever have son ask me how?
Books, Books, Books I will scream
Never a peasant for no one never no more
12:00 lunch time shot and a beer before
food, I don't know, never asked or did I.

Taste and drink drinks
only inhale food
time card punched back in, rope burning on pulley me
burning on the inside ladies wear gloves to hide once
beautiful hands.

Work, Work, Work,
Heading down the court on a fast break
wearing the colors of state on my back
carrying portrait of an artist in my hand
or my mind.
left the pail in the tub too long
besides it is time for dinner.

My old high school
Tuna fish sandwiches
on Friday
torn, mary, ray, betty
absent on Monday
The clock in homeroom
22 never working
the business teacher trying
to get in touch with his feminist soul
rolling joints under the bleachers
with my ear, neck hair cut
basketball coach wishes he had been a jar
head
English teacher a misplaced barbi doll
The mystery of sex
after seeing the girl who looks like a woman
with breasts
but, but, but,
maybe can play house.

Walking over a beaten path once

again-

through woods that provided
walking up the stairs to home
stronger as you get older not younger
Heidi the dog is not with me now
neither is my weak grip to climb trees
as the leaves have changed
my mind some more and more
the horizon to my left of the path
that I thought was a mountain is now
only a knoll
Heidi would scamper away
for I thought a long time
I crush the leaves now as I walk
the same ground with her sweetly
dreams
that she and I share
the uncrushed leaves and weak grip a
path
brought home to who it can belong

I tried to tell the daughter of the wife
of the Boss that her mother was concerned
about her cousin with all the lovely girls
in town who were her friends
he's having a fine time
the wife is having fantasies from her childhood
the bossman is worried how to take his
customers
I can not tell her convincingly that her mother
The wife of the bossman dreams for some real
meat
so do you, too, she said

Harry my friend came to the bar
had a drink with me
starch shirt on he's up
wondering who will be riding shotgun
with him later
on the dark roller coaster roads,
Harry is looking at me with eyes of blue print
on how he is going to get her good,
what's up tonight anything or you just
counting your quarters going into the
cash register:
no, no, no, just going home early to get some
sleep
As he walked out
to his last supper.

Sitting in the uncomfortable chair
watching Earl Wilson pitch against the
Yankees
day-dreaming for my chance to pitch just
once
knock, knock, knock, knock,
strange gray haired man
gunsmoke character
mom's at a funeral night
hello son big baritone voice
tool box and badge
she is not home
everything is fine for a Saturday here
we have to turn off the lights the bill is
not paid
Matt Dillon walked away.

Mother you died again tonight
your heavy set figure on dark shadow
couch again
I walked around the block once before you died
pall malls and the record American paper
ready for delivery as usual
approach the old frame house once more
dog motionless on the grass
all the cars that had shuffled you around
the town once or twice before were in front
wrong time of day for them
the closer I stepped the further I was
from them, entering the porch once again
dark hush mellow, knees weaken
my spines rocked as you looked me dead in the
eyes
I traveled that scene before now the scene stares
me in the eye
you died again tonight
everything gone now
the RECORD AMERICAN paper died that night,
too,
mom.

The sheriff came to the top of

the
stairs
another eviction notice from the
judge
a chubby face man with pink
cheeks
and catholic blue eyes twitching
my mother a slim 5'3" 210
pounds
curled her tongue
the sheriff knees knocked
she performed like a guest
conductor
the sheriff thought the cymbals
were
in front of him
he wiggled his ass out the door
sideways
the catholic blue eyes squinted
the door was on the way
to heaven.

Walking up the
street
with a man named
Dad
forward not further
crawling up my
throat
from my stomach
a periscope
did not locate
the picture of his
eyes
A life without his
blood
that dribble
backwards
into a secular
wrath.

The birds chirp a song over

my
mother's grave
early in the morning after the
saloon closed
my father who I have spent
more
time with while dead than
alive
lies to the right
the birds do not chirp that far
my stance is crooked
the leaves damp
orange sunrise sailor's
delight
my father was a sailor
most of time on his ass in a
poker game
my mother knows she is
buried
beside the old man
the old man does not where
he is
buried

My mother was a small dignified
Fat and half toothless poor woman
Trying to find underwear that
Would fit
They could never stay up
Walking up and down Pope Street
Always a journey for a cigarette
People would bitch
Her son's never bought a car to give her a
Ride
A Viet Nam bonus
A white Chevy impala
Sons did not meet for a car on any day
She cracked if you where immigrants
I have a car
Come rain sleet snow ice sunshine
Up and down
Pope Street
Cigarette's or no Cigarette
She walked and got fatter
Cried over the fried potatoes
While the fetus's of dead kittens laid in the
gutter
Our window not moving again
Patrick the cat followed us at night
Into the streets of no light

As the house got dark from
our minds
quiet as ever the walls had been
we brought a body to a little town
far from the south side of Chicago
we laid him under trees and grass
all my mother said was that if he
knew
he was laid to rest under the sun
and a hill with grass
he'd be rolling over in his grave looking
for
the first place to have a drink.

Being Home

My mother turned her head
as she said, "What happened"
the voice was strange and far
away
I heard my mother's tears for the
first time
hearing a dog of love
cry for the first time
the old man had died
some one she had not seen but
heard
for eleven years or so
a brother at Paris Island
a brother at LackLand
a brother at the Abbey
Mother snapped a polaroid.

This poem is dedicated to JH, SH & JS for their commitment to justice.

The dark gravel parking lot

On the West side of the pit

Where gladiators collide

A devil on four wheels surveyed

The air with a sickle

Innocence kills as the gray clouds circle

With no eyes

Driving to another act of futility
Flashed the appearance of the devil
On four wheels hiding under the
Whirling winds, clouds, seeking direction
From the prey

My four wheels glided to the front

The smell of evil lit my nostrils
The eyeballs like laser connected with
The antenna of the devil

We pierced each other without solution

As the attempted prey walked alone to

Freedom

We challenged the empty shark eyes of the inner
vessels Of a heart with no blood

Our eight wheels move apart
One set to sunlight
One set to darkness
On a road traveled by innocence
We meet again on the same road to freedom
With people who seek
The one human being

(continued on pg 71)

Not seen
On a dark night of the wet Valley
Immeasurable the darkness of weakness
Clouded by a clogged antenna

The agents of free world descend
Like daddy long leg spiders
To conquer the quest

Many arms
Many eyes
Many tongues
Many keyboard clacks
Many cerebral vouerger

Oh where could the devil of evil snatch the innocence child

Of God

December the magic of determination
The sky opens up to retrieve the black hole
Of the past
A cold brisk dark day of being on a empty night

Eyes to seek
Eyes to declare
Eyes to eliminate
Eyes to look through
Eyes that were not there
To put a human behind the living and the invisible

The four wheel monster surface
In all of its flames and the cloistered Black Devil
Who commandeered the ship of death

A day again in the pit where gladiators collide the black hole of
numbers shouted The messengers of God shouted we were free of
the devil of evil

Yes Brook we met the devil who captured you for the dark evil of
your life

Our eyes, mind, arms now control him for the future not the past

The day the devil of evil went fishing no one bit

The devil of evil captured your innocence

Not you

Epilogue

Bob Clifford has written a powerful and unique book of poems about growing up and living with the past. The poems are about childhood and "the night passage of youth," and about the difficult and sometimes lonely process of becoming an adult. They are poems of memory, "walking over a beaten path once more," shaped around memories of the past and of an earlier self - memories of home, neighborhood and family. The author is Boston Irish and the poems evoke a strong sense of place and of a background of home and family and neighborhood. Although many of these are rooted in memory, these are not pastorals in any sense of the word, but are located in the unglamorous urban locales of the author's home ground - the cluttered streets, the gas stations, the bar-rooms and diners in Brookline, the old High School. Here are the scenes of youth and young adulthood, where the boy grew up and learned about life and death and language. They are scenes of instruction, outside and occasionally inside the classroom, where the social and economic divisions on the street were replicated, and where "the odd ones sat in front."

If the poems revolve around home and the people at home, around a mother who loved her son, they are also about leaving home, and about travelling west away from all that is known. They are poems set on the buses, trains and automobiles that shuttle you from the home to the workplace, about hitching a ride on Route 9, and about being on a train surrounded by "people from another life." It is about people who are far from home like the man who is thumbing a lift to get away from the routine, or about the emigrant boy who had travelled from a village and who drowned in a dark lake, 3,000 miles from home. When you leave home where is home? If you go back to what was home will it still be there? If the house burns down? If your people die, does the home live on? Has the phone number changed? The book contains many splendid things including elegies, for the mother, and for the father, whose footsteps he sometimes feels he is following.

72

The speaker's voice is honest, informal, direct and sometimes rather blunt. He speaks with tough and gritty candor, in a marvelously eloquent shorthand, delivered with a caustic intelligence, and very off-the-cuff. He makes it up as he goes along and he tells it like it is. This is that the great American poet Alan Dugan meant when he said of Bob Clifford's early poetry that it is courageous and frank and that "he is able to make the language of where he came from into the kind of poetry that only a tough man can get away with." The voice can sound colloquial, but can rise to passages of great elegance and lyricism. Many of the poems begin in medias res, without explanation, back-story or stage-setting, but they draw you into the speaker's world and personality. There is a sense of the speaker telling a story which in turn contains many other stories that he has heard regaled on the street. You know these poems have roots in autobiography but like the best poetry they rise above the personal and take on a courageous power of their own. These are poems of great distinctiveness and the book has a rare honesty and elegance all its own.

Jonathan Allison
Professor of English
University of Kentucky

A
special
thanks to
the philosophers
of the dowtown athletic,
club, Cloud Davidson, Ray and
Kelly Cihak, Randy Perkins, Kevin
Boyle, Chris Costas. Bob (ZMAN) Zarzar,
Greg (the mayor of downtown) Little, and to Chris
Gray for his specific observation of the layout of the poems.

Edited by Jonathan Allison at University of Kentucky
and Greg Johnson of Cambridge Massachusettes
The cover art and portrait of Robert on the back cover
are by Jesse Beam. The words from Alan Dugan on
the back cover are a reprinted quote from 1980.
The typeface is Times New Roman
Regular and is 60 pound paper. All
inquiries and correspondances can
be sent via email to
clifforb62@gmail
.com